MASON MEETS A MASON BEE

AN EDUCATIONAL ENCOUNTER WITH A POLLINATOR

DAWN PAPE

PRAISE *for* <u>MASON MEETS A MASON BEE</u>

"This is a cute tale ... about a boy who meets a bee and each of them is afraid of the other. The bee explains that it is a mason bee and does not want to sting, but pollinates plants to make food for people. Mason also gets to hear about insecticides and other issues for beneficial insects.

There are lovely colourful photos on every page. At the end are lessons and more detailed information for adults. This would be good for a class nature table or a family reading session and should help to educate young people about nature."
— *Claire O'Beara, award-winning fiction and non–fiction author*

"This book is a dynamite teaching tool and a must for schools, libraries, garden centers, grandparents and parents--and anyone else who likes to eat. Bursting with critical and timely information about the importance of pollinators, this lovely picture storybook delights, motivates and informs the reader. As gardeners become aware of the myriad of bees in their backyard, learning about common and wonderful pollinators like the mason bee is a must. The interplay of the pictures and words illustrate big topics in an understandable way-teaching young gardeners that there ARE gentle bees in the backyard and we shouldn't be afraid of them. They are necessary for growing our food!"
— *Dave Hunter, Crown Bees*

"Pape does a wonderful job addressing the common fear of children (and adults) that bees are aggressive and should be avoided. By focusing on a mason bee, she highlights the differences between these solitary bees and honey bees. This book is a fantastic introduction to the world of wild bees and pollination for children, and an excellent tool for parents to learn more about wild bees and why they need our collective help.

Mason Meets a Mason Bee is a delightful story about a young boy (Mason) who meets a talking mason bee. The mason bee helps Mason overcome his fear of insects (and bee stings) and shows him how he pollinates flowers, providing the fruit and vegetables that Mason likes to eat. The bee also conveys to Mason how he can help the bee thrive by planting native plants throughout the growing season."
— *Heather Holm, author of* <u>Pollinators of Native Plants</u>

"A wonderful story about a boy and a bee with the same name. The bee educates the boy and the reader on the importance of insects in our world. This was a fun, fact filled book that lets everyone who reads it know what they can do to help take care of our planet."
— *Cindy Musslewhite, Goodreads Five-Star Review*

"*Mason Meets a Mason Bee* by Dawn Pape is a book that should be on bookshelves and classrooms everywhere. It is about Mason who is afraid of bees. One day he meets a mason bee and learns that bees are also afraid of people. This book is a fun and educational way learning about bees. It is told in a rhyming way, it's informative and done in such a cute way. A great read aloud. This book is also a good teaching tool and in the back of the book you will find science lessons. The illustrations are clear and bright and the colors really stand out. I gave this book 5 stars but it truly deserves many more. I highly recommend this book to everyone and anyone who has young children or work with young children. I look for more by Dawn Pape."
— *Marjorie Boyd-Springer, Net Galley Review*

A delightful story with a serious real-life message, MASON MEETS A MASON BEE photographically illustrates the encounter of a young boy named MASON, with a type of bee [New to me!] which daily pollinated 100 times the amount of a honeybee. This particular Mason bee is both verbal and voluble, and instructs his namesake on several important lawn and garden matters.

The book also appends explanations, research, and links. The author, Dawn Pape, is the Lawn Chair Gardener.
— *Mallory Heart Reviews, Five-Star Review*

DEDICATION
and
INTRODUCTION

This book is dedicated to you and the beloved children in your life.
Their future is in our hands.

There are definitely big concepts and big words introduced in this little book. That's exactly what makes the book work so well for a wide audience. Even though the book looks and reads like a picture book for early elementary students, the science and social concepts are big enough for adults to ponder.
Enjoy the book and keep in touch!
Dawn Pape

Facebook	https://www.facebook.com/lawnchairgardener/
Twitter	@LawnChairGarden
Email	Dawn@LawnChairGardener.com
Website	LawnChairGardener.com

· ·

Photos were taken by the author with these exceptions:

Dave Hunter, Crown Bees (crownbees.com)
    p. 11, 13, 20, 27 close-up of male mason bee
    p. 10 mason bee on finger
    p. 15 mason bee covered in pollen
Dave M, Bee Diverse (beediverse.com)
    p. 25 bees on dandelion

Heather Holm, Pollinators of Native Plants
(pollinatorsnativeplants.com)
    cover (right)
    p. 9, 15 (right) mason bees in flight
    p. 12, 14, 15, 22 mason bee on flowers
Shutterstock
    p. 15 spraying plant
    p. 20 illustration of many bees

Fifth Edition: February 20, 2015
ISBN: 978-0-9851877-5-0
Printed in the United States of America

GOOD GREEN LIFE
—publishing—

P.O. Box 74
Circle Pines, MN 55014-1793

"Wait a minute," said the boy, "You're afraid of me? How could that be?"

"Well, of course I'm afraid," said the bee, "and I think it's wise!"
Have you noticed your giant size?"

Then the boy said, "But you can *sting*."

Frustrated, the normally nice bee hollered back in a BIG angry voice,
"But I rarely do—THAT'S THE THING!"

"I keep to myself. I don't want any strife.
I just want to visit flowers and live my own life.

The wasps and hornets give us native bees a bad name.
But I promise you, not all flying insects are the same.
I'm a gentle mason bee and . . ."

"**WAIT!**" said the boy, "**A MASON BEE?**
My name is **MASON** too!"
"Well," said the bee,
"it's sure nice to meet you."

"I've never met a bee before," said Mason, "I've always thought bees were vicious."

The bee replied, "And *I've* never met a human either. I've always thought people were malicious."

"Malicious?" asked Mason. "You know," explained the bee, "trying to hurt me."

"No, I don't know what you mean," said the boy, "People are nice. What you're telling me sounds fictitious."

To that the bee replied, "I wish I were just making up a tale
but the truth is you people are making us sick and frail.

Spray, spray, spray!
People use pesticides to keep **ALL** bugs away.

I know that some bugs are a hairy, scary bother,
but most bugs are *good*. Don't believe me? Go ask your father."

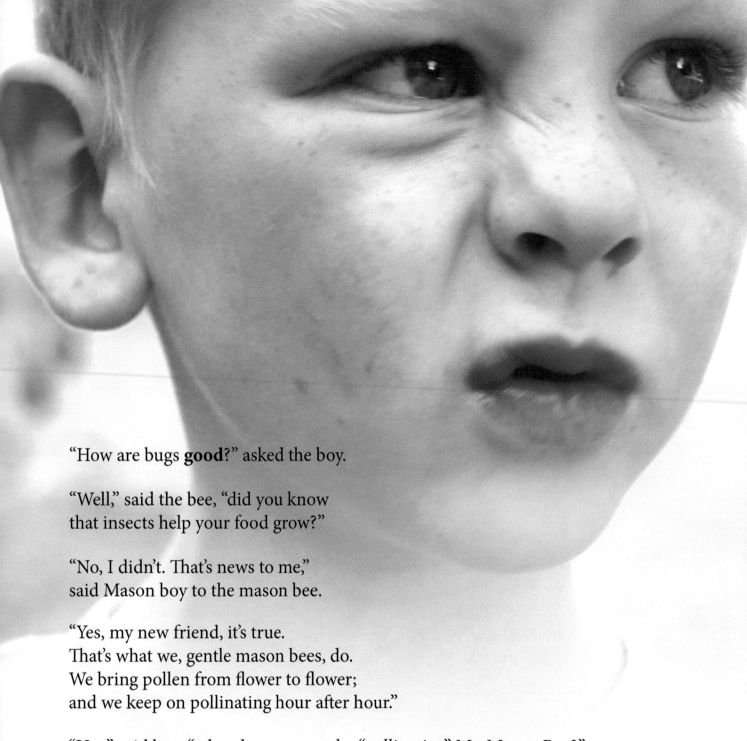

"How are bugs **good**?" asked the boy.

"Well," said the bee, "did you know
that insects help your food grow?"

"No, I didn't. That's news to me,"
said Mason boy to the mason bee.

"Yes, my new friend, it's true.
That's what we, gentle mason bees, do.
We bring pollen from flower to flower;
and we keep on pollinating hour after hour."

"Um," said boy, "what do you mean by "*pollinating*" Mr. Mason Bee?"

"POLLINATING," said bee,
"MEANS POLLEN DELIVERY.
Come watch! You'll see.

Look how I do a belly flop right onto this blossom.
I cover my whole belly with pollen—it's awesome.

Then loaded with pollen grains, to the next flower I fly,
the pollen rubs off and I've become the pollen delivery guy!"

*Actually, female mason bees collect pollen
and do most of the pollinating,
but that doesn't have the same ring to it, does it?*

"Sorry," said Mason, "but I still don't see
what delivering pollen has to do with growing food for me."

The bee explained, "Pollen from one flower helps seeds inside another flower grow."

"**OHHHHH!**" exclaimed Mason, "And the seeds grow into the **FOOD** we eat!
I get it now. That's super duper neat."

"Yes," said bee, "peas and beans, cherries and berries,
cucumbers and squash. . .
The list goes on and on, oh my gosh!"

Summer squash flower growing into a summer squash

Summer squash ready to be picked!

"So," said the boy, "the next time I sit down for lunch,
I will thank you a bunch!"

"Thank you," said bee,
"but it's not just me—

remember the butterflies, moths, wasps and flies.
Even beetles help pollinate to many people's surprise.

Don't get me wrong, I do enjoy the praise
because there is currently a bit of a honey bee craze."

The bee continued, "One thing that troubles me so
is that **_all bees_** are important to the world and people just don't know!

Honey bees get most of the attention and fame.
Just because they make honey everyone knows **_their_** name.
But my pollination skills are tremendous. I put honey bees to shame.

As a mason bee, I'm proud to say,
I pollinate as much as **100*** honey bees on any given day."

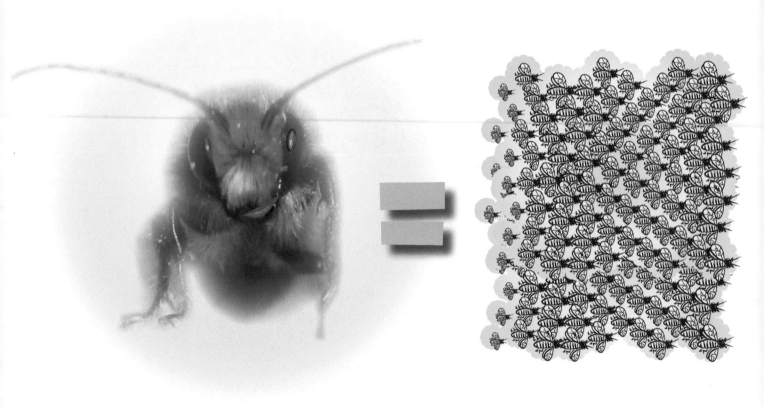

** Mason bees are great pollinators because they cover their entire "bellies"
with pollen whereas most bees only carry pollen with their hind legs.*

Mason exclaimed, "Wow! As much as 100 honey bees? That's so cool.
I can hardly wait to tell my friends at school."

"I am sorry, Mr. Mason Bee, that people are hurting you.
Tell me, what should I do?"

"That's easy," said the bee, "Just make good choices.
You need to speak for us, because insects have no voices."*

* Except me. I am a special mason bee who can talk.

"What kind of choices?" asked Mason.

"Tell your parents to avoid plants with pesticides in the soil from the store.
And heaven forbid, don't apply more!

In your garden, a little insect damage is OK;
there is really no need to spray."

"Is there anything else you would like to teach me,
Mr. Mason Bee?"

"Why, yes! When people build their houses, they take away ours.
It would be very kind if you could plant us some flowers."

"Sure," said Mason boy,
"What kind of flowers do you enjoy?"

The bee replied enthusiastically, "Locally grown natives!
Cultivars* with little nectar and pollen really aren't the greatest."

* A "cultivar" is short for "cultivated variety" and is a plant
engineered for certain traits such as unique bloom colors.

"And to some people, what I am about to say may be considered treason,
but I think of dandelions as spring **FLOWERS**—not weeds—and I'll tell you the reason.

There isn't much blooming early in the year
and every day it's starvation I fear."

"S-t-a-r-v-a-t-i-o-n?" repeated the boy slowly in disbelief, "Oh, dear."

"All growing season long," said bee, "I hope your blooms last
to help us eat every day, because bees really don't like to fast.

You feed me and I'll return the favor.
I'll pollinate yummy apples for you to savor."

Pasque Flower
Blooms Early in the Spring

Golden Alexander
Blooms in the Spring

Blue Flag Iris
Blooms in the Spring

Butterfly Weed (or Flower)
Blooms Early in the Summer

Yellow Coneflower
Blooms Mid-Late Summer

Prairie Blazing Star
Blooms Mid-Late Summer

Purple Coneflower
Blooms Mid-Late Summer

New England Aster
Blooms in the Fall

Then the boy said with concern, "Mason bee, don't you worry,
People are nice. Once they understand your problems, they will change their ways in a hurry!"

"Goodbye and thank you, Mason boy.
Our time together was a joy.
I look forward to seeing you later."
"Yes!" said Mason, "See you later, pollinator!"

The bee's reply? "After awhile . . .
compost pile!"

"Compost pile? Whaat!" laughed Mason, "Toodeloo
—and right back at you."

As Mason turned and waved,
he was feeling strong and brave;
of bees he was no longer afraid.

In fact, he felt like a superhero because he knew
he had an extremely important job to do.

HE IS GOING TO HELP PROTECT THE BEES! ARE YOU?

> "Treat the earth well: it was not given to you by your parents,
> it was loaned to you by your children."—Kenyan Proverb

A Little More Information about Mason Bees

I hope the kids reading this book want to run right outside and find a mason bee after finishing it. However, so your kids aren't disappointed, please note that mason bees are only active in the spring—and they're fast and hard to see too! But, there are many other kinds of solitary bees that are active at other times of year.

Let's Talk about the Birds and the Bees—and their Declining Populations

Perhaps it seems a little inappropriate to discuss the "birds and the bees" in a children's book, but we all know that this is a pivotal topic. Birds, bees and other pollinating insects' "deeds" of transferring pollen from the male flower parts to the female flower parts resulting in fertilization and the production of seeds is an invaluable service. Think about the labor costs if we had to pay workers to do this to produce our fruits and vegetables! It's true that some crops are pollinated by birds, bats and even wind, but most rely on pollinating insects—especially bees. The problem is, pollinators are in peril with a few huge strikes against them. According University of Minnesota researcher Marla Spivak, managed bee colonies are experiencing unsustainable annual losses around 30 percent of their population since the winter of 2006-2007. Native bee populations are harder to track, but are also in decline.

Why are Bee Populations Declining?

Habitat loss and broad-spectrum insecticides (especially applied to plants in bloom) are known causes for declining bee populations. Logically, as human populations increase, land is developed for "people spaces" such as houses, schools, shopping, etc. Subsequently, a leading "crop" in the U.S. is now lawn grass, providing very little habitat for pollinators. Another factor in declining habitat involves changing farming practices with fewer buffers of native wildflowers. On top of habitat loss, insecticide use is prevalent and bee kills are a common side-effect of crop dusting and mosquito control programs.

A particular class of insecticides, neonicotinoids, that was introduced in mid-1990s, is noteworthy. This class of chemicals is related to nicotine and attacks the insects' nervous systems. Neonicotinoids, also called neonics, are systemic, meaning they permeate the whole plant, including the nectar and pollen and they persist for a long time unlike other insecticides. The neonicotinoids do not kill the insects on contact, but impair the insects' abilities to navigate back to their hives or nests. Bees feed on the nectar and bring pollen back to their brood slowly weakening the whole colony or nest with these neuro-toxins and making the bees more susceptible to disease. These pesticides are suspected in contributing to bees dying of viruses and may help explain "colony collapse disorder." Neonics are commonly used in potting soil by growers. Thankfully, new 2014 labeling laws with a "bee advisory box" require growers to label their plants if neonics are present.

How Can You Help?

Please give yourself a pat on the back because you already have helped protect bees by educating the kids in your life about the big topics in this little book. Here are some other ways to help...

Vote with Your Dollars

The new labeling laws are a good start, but consumers need to keep paying attention and demand transparency in labeling seeds, plants and products.

Create Pollinator Habitat and Nesting Sites

Plant a native garden. Plant an array of native plants with different flower shapes that bloom in succession throughout your entire growing season to support a variety of pollinators. To learn more about planting a native plant garden, visit BlueThumb.org.

If gardening isn't your forte, consider just **keeping some soil bare** in your yard. Many native bees are ground nesters and need bare, loose soil. Another way to support bees is learn how to keep honey bees or maintain bee houses for mason bees.

Reduce Chemical Use

When feasible, buy organic food, try growing (at least some of) your own food and eliminate chemical use in your own yard. If you need help getting started, *A Lawn Chair Gardener's Guide to a Balanced Life and World* may be a helpful book for you.

Speak for the Bees

If you are still feeling energetic, please help get the word out about these important topics while raising money for your organization or retail location by selling this book (and others). Your organization's profit is 55% of the retail price. Get started by visiting www.GoodGreenLifePublishing.com.

Books and Websites to Learn More about Insects and Habitat

Bee Lab (beelab.umn.edu)

Bee research at the University of Minnesota intended to promote the health of bees. Learn more about honey bees and solitary bees.

Beez Kneez (www.thebeezkneezdelivery.com/education)

Wear a beekeeping suit, look inside a bee hive, meet the queen, taste honey and learn about the bee situation. Classes (aka a work retreat, field trip or birthday party) are held at a Beez Kneez Urban Apiary Partner Site, a community garden, urban farm, park or school close to you.

Blue Thumb—*Planting for Clean Water* (bluethumb.org)

Designed to make it easy for homeowners to plan, purchase and plant native gardens, raingardens, and shoreline stabilization to reduce polluted stormwater runoff from their home landscape in an effort improve water quality and wildlife habitat.

Crown Bees (crownbees.com)

Learn how to keep mason bees. Subscribe to "Bee-Mail" for helpful seasonal information.

Garden at School (gardenatschool.wordpress.com)

Tips for engaging kids with gardening activities, pollination games, seed dispersal lessons, parts of plants, scavenger hunts, composting and more...

Good Bug, Bad Bug, by Jessica Walliser

Useful book about "Who's Who, What They Do and How to Manage Them Organically (All You Need to Know about the Insect in Your Garden)

Monarch Watch (monarchwatch.org)

Dedicated to education, conservation, and research of the Monarch butterfly.

Pollinators of Native Plants, by Heather Holm

Important book for gardeners, native plant enthusiasts, landscape restoration professionals or anyone interested in attracting, identifying, supporting or planting for pollinators.

Pollinator Partnership—*Your Source for Pollinator Action and Information* (pollinator.org)

The largest organization in the world dedicated exclusively to the protection and promotion of pollinators and their ecosystems. Extensive PreK-12 curriculum.

Restoring the Landscape (restoringthelandscape.com)

Blog created as a resource for homeowners in the Midwestern and Northeastern states and provinces to help with all aspects of restoring one's landscape.

Xerces Society (xerces.org)

Dedicated to protecting wildlife through the conservation of invertebrates and their habitat.

CPSIA information can be obtained
at www.ICGtesting.com
Printed in the USA
LVHW071206251118
598196LV00013B/1476/P

* 9 780985 187750 *